THE OLYMPICS

GREAT OLYMPIC MOMENTS

HAYDN MIDDLETON

The Olympic Spirit

The modern Olympic Games began in 1896. Since then the Games' organizers have tried to ensure that every competitor keeps to the true Olympic spirit. This spirit is based on fair play, international friendship, a love of sport purely for its own sake, and the ideal that it is more important to take part than to win.

Heinemann Library
Des Plaines, Illinois

Designed by AMR
Originated by Dot Gradations
Printed in Hong Kong/China

04 03 02 01 00
10 9 8 7 6 5 4 3 2 1

Library of Congress Cataloging-in-Publication Data
Middleton, Haydn.
    Great Olympic moments / Haydn Middleton.
        p. cm. – (Olympics)
    Includes bibliographical references (p.) and index.
    Summary: Explores some of the greatest moments and personalities of
the Olympics, from the inception of the modern games in 1896 through
the present.
    ISBN 1-57572-451-0 (library binding)
    1. Olympics—History Juvenile literature. [1. Olympics-
-History.] I. Title. II. Series: Middleton, Haydn. Olympics.
GV721.53.M54 1999
796.48—dc21   99-24331
                                                                     CIP

Acknowledgments
The Publishers would like to thank the following for permission to reproduce
photographs: Allsport, pp. 6, 7, 8, 9, 10, 11, 12, 13, 14, 15, 18, 20, 21, 22, 24, 25, 26,
28, 29; Colorsport, pp. 16, 19; Corbis/Bettmann, p. 23; Empics, p. 17; Hulton Getty, p. 27.

Cover photograph reproduced with permission of Bob Martin, Allsport.

Every effort has been made to contact copyright holders of any material reproduced in
this book. Any omissions will be rectified in subsequent printings if notice is given to the
Publisher.

Any words appearing in the text in bold, **like this**, are explained in the
Glossary.

Contents

Introduction

The modern Olympics began in 1896. Every Games since then has been lit up by marvelous sporting moments. The Olympic motto is *Citius, Altius, Fortius*. This is Latin for "swifter, higher, stronger." This book is about the runners, jumpers, swimmers, gymnasts, skiers, and soccer players who lived and played by that motto. Sometimes these men and women achieved success with style and ease. Sometimes they fought against terrific odds to come out on top. All of them won lasting, worldwide fame.

The joy of taking part

For competitors and spectators alike, nothing quite compares with the thrill of an Olympic final. Britain's Sebastian Coe knows that as well as anyone. In 1980 and again in 1984 he won the gold medal for the 1,500-meter run. "There may be championships galore," he wrote later, "but to every young athlete who tied on his or her first pair of spikes in a drafty clubhouse in Sheffield, or at a high school track in Baltimore, or in a corrugated-roofed changing room in Nairobi, it is the Olympic finals that matter."

The Olympic Games also have a second, unofficial motto, adapted from an American bishop's sermon in 1908. It describes what could be called the true Olympic spirit. "The most important thing in the Olympic Games is not to win, but to take part, just as the most important thing in life is not the triumph, but the struggle. The essential thing is not to have conquered, but to have fought well."

Great Olympic champions live by the motto, "Swifter, Higher, Stronger."

This motto might seem hard to believe today. In our world, winning often seems to mean everything, and finishing second is often portrayed in the **media** as failure. But second place doesn't need to mean failure, as in the following Olympic story.

From me to you

Czech distance runner Emil Zatopek was one of the greatest Olympians of all. In the early 1950s no one could match him. At the Helsinki Games of 1952 he won three gold medals. Then in the 1960s another magnificent distance runner emerged— Ron Clarke of Australia. Everyone knew Clarke was the world's best, and he had the records to prove it. Even though he gave his all at Tokyo in 1964 and again at Mexico City in 1968, he was without a single Olympic victory.

On his way back to Australia in 1968, he stopped in Europe to see his old friend, Emil Zatopek. Zatopek gave Clarke a small gift, which Clarke opened when he returned home. Inside was Zatopek's gold medal for winning the 10,000-meter run in 1952. Olympian Sebastian Coe pointed out the following: "Zatopek, the kindest of men, well knew the important difference between failure and not winning. In that sense Ron Clarke had not failed, and the Olympic Games were richer for him." In the pages that follow are the stories of many others who have truly enriched the Olympics.

SITES OF THE MODERN OLYMPIC GAMES

Year	Summer Games	Winter Games
1896	Athens, Greece	—
1900	Paris, France	—
1904	St. Louis, Missouri	—
1908	London, England	—
1912	Stockholm, Sweden	—
1916	Games not held	—
1920	Antwerp, Belgium	—
1924	Paris, France	Chamonix, France
1928	Amsterdam, Netherlands	St. Moritz, Switzerland
1932	Los Angeles, California	Lake Placid, New York
1936	Berlin, Germany	Garmisch-Partenkirchen, Germany
1940	Games not held	Games not held
1944	Games not held	Games not held
1948	London, England	St. Moritz, Switzerland
1952	Helsinki, Finland	Oslo, Norway
1956	Melbourne, Australia	Cortina d'Ampezzo, Italy
1960	Rome, Italy	Squaw Valley, California
1964	Tokyo, Japan	Innsbruck, Austria
1968	Mexico City, Mexico	Grenoble, France
1972	Munich, West Germany	Sapporo, Japan
1976	Montreal, Canada	Innsbruck, Austria
1980	Moscow, **USSR**	Lake Placid, New York
1984	Los Angeles, California	Sarajevo, Yugoslavia (now Bosnia-Herzegovina)
1988	Seoul, South Korea	Calgary, Canada
1992	Barcelona, Spain	Albertville, France
1994	—	Lillehammer, Norway
1996	Atlanta, Georgia	
1998	—	Nagano, Japan
2000	Sydney, Australia	—
2002	—	Salt Lake City, Utah
2004	Athens, Greece	—

The Winter Games were not held until 1924. Since 1992 the Summer and Winter Games have been held on a staggered two-year schedule.

The Fastest Men in the World

For many sports fans, nothing can beat the excitement of the two great Olympic sprint races, the 100-meter run and the 200-meter run. The first Olympic 100-meter run champion was Thomas Burke of the United States. He won the 1896 race in Athens in a time of 12 seconds. One hundred years later, in Atlanta, Georgia, Canadian Donovan Bailey won the gold medal in the same event with a time of 9.84 seconds.

Until 1924, Americans won every 100-meter run title except one. All these winners were white men, but more and more black athletes were becoming great Olympians. At Los Angeles in 1932 Thomas Eddie Tolan, an African American sprinter from the University of Michigan, won gold in both the 100-meter run and the 200-meter run. Four years later, the next Olympic sprint champion was perhaps the greatest sprinter ever to run.

In 1936 Jesse Owens was asked for the secret of his success by a London reporter. He replied, "I let my feet spend as little time as possible on the ground. From the air, fast down, and from the ground, fast up. My foot is only a fraction of the time on the track."

In later years, Jesse Owens became involved in community service. He believed that athletic competitions could help solve racial and political problems.

Enter Jesse Owens

By the time of the 11th Games in 1936, Jesse Owens was already a living legend. The year before, at an American championship, he broke three world records and tied a fourth, all in the space of 45 minutes.

News of this fabulous feat stunned the world. But surely he would have a hard job living up to everyone's expectations at the Olympics in Berlin, Germany.

Germany's ruling **Nazi** Party was trying hard to convince anyone who would listen that athletes from what they called the white German master race were superior to athletes of any other race. They saw the Olympic Games as an opportunity to demonstrate their racist theory.

But Jesse Owens, an African American, proved himself to be unbeatable at the 100-meter run, the 200-meter run, the long jump, and the sprint relay. In the words of one rival, he made it all look as easy as water running downhill. At the time, few people would have guessed that Owens' achievement of winning four gold medals would ever be equaled at a later Games. But in 1984, it was matched by another African American, Carl Lewis.

From crutches to glory

Carl Lewis was small as a child, but he began to grow at the age of fifteen. He grew so fast that he had to use crutches for three weeks while his body adjusted. In 1984 at Los Angeles, Lewis won gold medals in exactly the same four events that Jesse Owens won. Owens had won the 100-meter run in 10.3 seconds. Lewis won it in 9.92 seconds, eight feet ahead of his next opponent. It was the widest winning margin in Olympic history.

Carl Lewis of the United States was not just a world-record beating sprinter, but a fabulous long-jumper, too. In Atlanta, Geogia, in 1996, he won the Olympic long jump for the fourth time.

In 1988 in Seoul, South Korea, Lewis retained his 100-meter run and long jump titles. No man had ever done that before. But Lewis managed only a second-place silver medal in the 200-meter run. He was not finished, though. In Barcelona in 1992 he picked up his seventh and eighth gold medals in the long jump and the 4 × 100-meter relay. By the age of 23, Lewis was already earning $1 million a year from commercial endorsements, even though he still held **amateur** status.

Fabulous Finns

The United States holds the top spot on the Olympic all-time medals chart. This is not suprising, because the Unites States has always taken the training of its athletes very seriously. Its **Cold War** rival, the **USSR,** which holds second place for total medals, turned the making of Olympic champions into an industry. The next spots are held by several European nations, such as Germany and Italy, which have a long history of sporting excellence. But just behind these countries is a rather surprising country—Finland.

Lasse Viren (in front) was one of a long line of great Finnish distance runners.

The driving force of *sisu*

Between 1912 and 1936, Finland's track athletes won 24 gold medals. This was an extraordinary achievement for a nation that even now numbers only five million people. A second great age of Olympic success opened up for the Finns at Munich in 1972. Then, as before, the Finns did well in long and middle distance running.

Why was this? The Finns talk of a national characteristic called *sisu*. This is a single-minded mixture of pride and guts and the will to win. Perhaps Finnish victories had something to do with *sisu*.

At the 1912 Games in Stockholm, there was no independent country called Finland. It was still a part of the Russian Empire. Its athletes ran under the Russian flag. That did not stop smiling Hannes Kolehmainen, a vegetarian bricklayer, from winning the 5,000- and 10,000-meter runs, and the cross-country race.

Finnish flyers

From 1920 to 1928, a carpenter's son, Paavo Nurmi, was so far ahead of his rivals that his main challenge came from beating his own previous time. In fact, he carried a stopwatch while he ran, to improve his pace judgment. Nurmi won nine Olympic gold medals and broke 22 official world records in distances ranging from 1,500 meters to 20,000 meters. When he no longer competed, other distance runners kept Finland high in the medals table until the outbreak of World War II. Then amazingly, from 1948 to 1972, the Finns did not win a single Olympic title. The man who changed all that was another **phenomenon** of the track, Lasse Viren.

Viren was a 23-year-old policeman. He won his first gold medal at Munich the hard way. In the middle of the 10,000-meter run finals, Viren stumbled and fell. One of his main rivals, Muhammad Gammoudi, tripped on him, crashed to the ground, and left the race shortly after that. Viren, on the other hand, got up and continued on, all the way to the gold medal. He set a new world record time of 27 minutes 36.35 seconds. He then won the 5,000-meter run, too. At Montreal, four years later, he repeated his double-gold performance and nearly won the marathon race as well! If any Finnish athlete had *sisu* to spare, it was Lasse Viren.

Distance running is not the only Finnish specialty. Finland's skiers and speed skaters make frequent visits to the medal podium at the Winter Games.

Finnish athletes also excel in the javelin throw. The men have won seven Olympic javelin throw titles since World War I.

In the women's event, Ilse Tiina Lillak set a world record to win the 1983 World Championship, but an injury kept her from competing at the Los Angeles Games in 1984.

Tiny Gymnastic Giants

The sport of gymnastics has figured in every modern Games since 1896. But, as in most Olympic sports, women's competitions took longer to arrive than men's. At Amsterdam in 1928 the first women's gymnastic team event took place. Then in 1952, women's individual apparatus was introduced. So the stage was set for some of the most memorable Olympic champions of all. Many of them came from the countries of eastern Europe.

Eastern European gold

At the 1972 Games, the world met the Munchkin of Munich. She was a petite seventeen-year-old gymnast from the **USSR** named Olga Korbut. She was only 4 feet 11 inches (150 centimeters) tall and weighed just 86 pounds (39 kilograms). Her mischievous smile entranced millions of people. She was also popular with the judges.

They awarded her three gold medals, even though some experts questioned her technique. Her teammate, nineteen-year-old Lyudmila Turischeva, won the all-around title. Four years later another young Soviet gymnast, Nelli Kim, received perfect scores of ten from two of the judges for her performances. Even so, she did not manage to win the all-around crown.

Olga Korbut was the darling of the world's **media** at Munich in 1972. When she went for a walk during the Games, buses stopped so that passengers could get out and ask for her autograph. On returning home to Grodno in the USSR, she got so much fan mail that a clerk was employed just to handle her incoming letters.

The champion that year in Montreal was Romania's awesome Nadia Comaneci. Only fourteen years of age, she had trained as a gymnast since the age of six. She scored tens from all seven judges on both the parallel bars and the balance beam. Unprepared for such a gymnastic genius, the electronic scoreboard could show nothing higher than 9.95. For Comaneci's performance, the scoreboard registered only 1.00. But she knew she had achieved perfection. Four years later, at the age of eighteen, she dazzled Moscow. Her final total of Olympic medals was nine. Five of them were gold.

Nadia Comaneci was the star of the 1976 Games. At press conferences in Montreal, journalists asked the shy fourteen-year-old what was her greatest wish. "I want to go home," she replied.

The older generation

Between 1956 and 1964, Soviet gymnast Larissa Latynina won 18 Olympic medals, more than any other Olympian in history. At the 1956 and 1960 Games, she won the all-around crown for female gymnasts. This feat was equaled only by Vera Caslavska of Czechoslovakia in 1964 and 1968. While Caslavska was famous for artistic expression, Latynina was technically superb. At Rome in 1960, Latynina was a young mother when she competed. She had recently given birth to a daughter, Tatiana. Tatiana grew up to be a well-known ballet dancer.

Leaps of the Century

Someone once said that Olympic records are like piecrusts—they are meant to be broken. Since 1896, more than 50 percent of the finals of **track and field** events have been won with record-breaking performances. The figure for swimming is greater than 70 percent. In some Olympic events, however, records tend to stand for a very long time. In the case of the men's long jump, it can seem like an eternity.

At Berlin in 1936, Jesse Owens set a new Olympic record of 26 feet 5 1/2 inches (8.06 meters) for the long jump. But he did not beat the world record he had set the year before in Michigan. On that day, just before he jumped, an announcer told the crowd, "Jesse Owens will now attempt a new long jump world's record." And he did it, with a leap of 26 feet 8 inches (8.13 meters)! His record stood until Ralph Boston of the United States broke it in 1960.

At the 1968 Mexico City Games, Bob Beamon jumped beyond the range of the officials' state-of-the-art measuring device. An old-fashioned steel tape had to be brought in to make the measurement.

Dizzy heights for long-jumpers

Before the Mexico City Games of 1968, everyone talked about the city's high **altitude**. They thought the thin air would have a bad effect on the breathing of long-distance runners. But no one predicted the good effect it would have on athletes in the more explosive events, such as the long jump.

Three medalists from the 1964 Tokyo Games, Lynn Davies (UK), Ralph Boston (USA), and Igor Ter-Ovanesyan (**USSR**) were all competing again. Each was in good enough physical shape to win the gold. But an outsider struggled through the qualifying round to compete against them in the final.

He was a 6 foot 3 inch (190 centimeters), 22-year-old New Yorker named Bob Beamon. He could run like the wind, but had great trouble in hitting the take-off board. He jumped fourth among seventeen finalists. With his first leap, he took long-jumping into a new dimension. After a perfect take-off, Beamon sailed high through the air. Then he hit the sand so hard that he bounced back up and landed outside the pit.

"You have destroyed this event."

How far did Beamon go? The electronic scoreboard showed a distance of 8.90 meters. But until the metric measurement was converted into feet and inches, Bob Beamon did not realize what a stupendous jump he had. No one in history had ever achieved a 28-foot jump. And still no one had, because the gangling American had bypassed 28 feet altogether and cleared 29 feet 2 1/2 inches! No one could hope to beat that. Long-jumper Lynn Davies said to the new champion, "You have destroyed this event." Davies was not quite right, because in 1991, Mike Powell finally surpassed Beamon's world-record mark in a non-Olympic competition. But the amazing jump of 1968 still stands as an Olympic record.

High jump flops

Unlike the long jump, the high jump was not an event in the ancient Greek Games. In modern Games it is often a breathtakingly exciting event. American Dick Fosbury changed the nature of the high jump forever in Mexico City when he won a gold medal with his new head-first and backwards style of clearing the bar. In 1968 the Fosbury Flop looked very risky. Fosbury's coach warned, "If kids imitate Fosbury, he will wipe out an entire generation of jumpers, because they will all have broken necks." In later years, the Fosbury Flop became the standard style for high jumpers.

Amazing Africans

Until 1960, no black African athlete had won a **track and field** gold medal. That all changed at the Rome Olympics when an Ethiopian bodyguard named Abebe Bikila made winning the marathon race look as easy as ABC.

Marathon marvel

The 1960 marathon was the first to be staged at night, when the temperature was cooler. It was also the first to start and end outside the stadium. This race would be only the third time Abebe Bikila had run a marathon in his life. But he won, running barefoot, in a time of 2 hours 15 minutes 16.2 seconds. His biggest challenge near the end came from a motorscooter rider who lurched onto the course by mistake.

Four years later, Bikila proved that his victory was no accident. Only 40 days before the Tokyo marathon, he had his appendix removed. He still finished first in a time of 2 hours 12 minutes 11.2 seconds. It was the fastest time ever recorded. He even ran a lap of honor before the next runner, Britain's Basil Heatley, appeared in the stadium.

Kenyan policeman Kipchoge Keino was the undisputed track star of the 1968 Games. As a boy he ran fifteen miles (24 kilometers) to and from school each day.

Africans at altitude

At Mexico City in 1968 another Ethiopian, 36-year-old Mamo Wolde, won the marathon. More than an hour after Wolde finished the race, John Akhwari of Tanzania finally entered the stadium. He had hurt himself badly in a fall, but struggled on through the pain. "My country did not send me 7,000 miles to start the race," he said afterward. "They sent me 7,000 miles to finish it."

Many African athletes lived and trained at high **altitudes**, so the Mexico City Games, held at more than 6,500 feet (2,000 meters) above sea level, held no terrors for them. At every race distance from 1,500 meters to the marathon, African runners took the gold medal. In the 5,000-meter run and 10,000-meter run, all three medalists came from Africa. In the first of those races, uncoached Kenyan Kipchoge Keino lost by a hair's breadth to Tunisia's Muhammad Gammoudi. In the 1,500-meter run, he went one place better, even though he had to run to the stadium before the race because he had been caught in a traffic jam.

Keino was up against world-record holder Jim Ryun of the United States. Keino was suffering from violent stomach pains. In spite of this, he won the gold by beating Ryun with the largest-ever margin of victory in this event. At Munich four years later, Keino won second place in the 1,500-meter run behind Pekka Vasala of Finland. Then to challenge himself, he entered the 3,000-meter steeplechase, too. In this event, which features 28 hurdles and 7 water jumps, Keino had little experience. He admitted that he jumped "like an animal." Still, he was good enough to win the gold medal and set an Olympic record time of 8 minutes 23.6 seconds.

At Barcelona in 1992 the women's 10,000-meter run was a race to remember. After the 6,000-meter mark, South African Elana Meyer took the lead. Derartu Tulu of Ethiopia led with her. Soon these two were so far ahead that no one else could catch them. Lap after lap Tulu ran just behind Meyer. Then with 420 meters to go, she eased in front, stormed away, and won by 30 meters (98 feet).

For the first time, a black African woman had won an Olympic medal. Meyer's silver medal was South Africa's first medal since South Africa had been banned from the Games. The two women shared the victory lap.

Soccer Stars

Until 1930, when the soccer World Cup competition began, the winners of the Olympic soccer tournament could rightly be called the champions of the world. Only five countries entered the first full tournament of the 1908 Games. England was the winner. The 1920 finals between host nation Belgium and Czechoslovakia ended with the Czech team walking off the field in the second half, because they felt that the referee was favoring the home team.

True world champions

At the 1924 Games in Paris, many Europeans were able to watch a dazzling South American team for the first time. That team was Uruguay, and they took the tournament by storm. They beat Switzerland 3–0 in the finals to take the gold medal.

OLYMPIC SOCCER CHAMPIONS

These are the all the winners since the first full Olympic soccer tournament in 1908:

1908 England
1912 England
1920 Belgium
1924 Uruguay
1928 Uruguay
1936 Italy
1948 Sweden
1952 Hungary
1956 **USSR**
1960 Yugoslavia
1964 Hungary
1968 Hungary
1972 Poland
1976 East Germany
1980 Czechoslovakia
1984 France
1988 USSR
1992 Spain
1996 Nigeria

In 1996 the first women's Olympic soccer tournament was held. It was won by the United States.

The last Olympic soccer champion who could also be called the true world champion was Hungary in 1952. Featuring stars like Hidegkuti, Koscis, and Puskas (on the left), they scored 20 goals and gave up only 2 goals in the 1952 tournament.

Virtually the same team then played in the 1954 World Cup Finals against West Germany. Earlier in the competition they had already thrashed the Germans 8–3. Yet to everyone's amazement, they managed to lose in the finals by a score of 2–3.

Four years later, in Amsterdam, the Uruguayans returned, accompanied by the Argentinians. The Argentinians thrashed the United States 11–2, beat Belgium 6–3, and then crushed Egypt 6–0 on the way to the finals. Then the Argentinians met Uruguay! After the first match ended in a tie, Uruguay won the replay 2–1 to retain their Olympic title. Few could doubt that they were the best team in the world.

In 1936 in Berlin, recent World Cup winner Italy also won the Olympic gold. By that time, so many of the world's best soccer players were **professional** that many nations sent understrength, **amateur** squads to the Olympics. During the **Cold War** period, the **communist** countries of eastern Europe dominated the tournament, combining skill with strong government support.

The United States women's soccer team won the first Olympic gold medal in women's soccer in 1996. They are shown here beating Norway in the semi-finals.

Professionals allowed in

After 1976, professional players who had not competed in World Cup games were allowed to take part in the Olympics. Soccer at the Games continued to draw in huge crowds. In 1984 and 1988 more spectators watched soccer than any other event. Then in 1992, at Barcelona, the rules changed again. The Olympic soccer tournament became the official competition for all the world's under-23-year-old teams.

Repeat Performances

To win a gold medal in any Olympic event is a supreme achievement. To go back four years later and win again is quite staggering. But to be the Olympic champion a third time and a fourth time seems almost unbelievable. It takes a very special person to be the world's best for sixteen years.

One-man gold rushes

Ray Ewry of the United States won a record ten gold medals between 1900 and 1908 in the now discontinued standing jumps. He won in spite of the fact that he had polio as a boy. Russian triple-jumper Viktor Saneyev won his event in 1968, 1972, and 1976. Then in 1980, at the age of 34, he failed by only 4 inches (11 centimeters) to add a fourth gold medal to his career total.

By then, one man had already achieved the stupendous feat of winning four gold medals. He was Paul Elvstrom of Denmark. He won his four consecutive gold medals in the Finn class of the yachting competitions between 1948 and 1960. At the Helsinki Games of 1952, he was so many points ahead that he did not have to race on the last day. But he entered anyway and won that race, too!

British rower Steve Redgrave won gold medals at four Olympic Games in a row. The official magazine of the International Olympic Committee pronounced him "Rower of the Century."

In Atlanta in 1996, he won the pairs event with Matthew Pinsent. He is now in training to try for a fifth consecutive gold medal at the Sydney Games in the year 2000.

The ultimate competitor

Only two athletes have ever won the same Olympic **track and field** event four times. One was Carl Lewis, who won the long jump four times between 1984 and 1996. The other was discus thrower Al Oerter in 1956, 1960, 1964, and 1968. When he won his first gold medal with a new Olympic record, the truth did not sink in until he was up on the victory **rostrum**. Then his knees buckled, and he almost fell off.

Oerter was more than just a great thrower, he was a great competitor. Three times he had to beat the current world-record holder to win gold. Three times he produced a lifetime-best throw to set the winning mark. At Tokyo in 1964, he injured his lower ribs so badly while practicing, that doctors told him to forget about competing. But it took more than that to stop him. With his fifth throw, he doubled up in pain, but still set a new Olympic record to win the event. "These are the Olympics," the hero explained afterward. "You die for them."

Britain's Francis "Daley" Thompson won the grueling **decathlon** twice, first in 1980 and again in 1984. His point total in Los Angeles has not been beaten at any Games since. British Olympic 800-meter run champion Steve Ovett called the decathlon "nine Mickey Mouse events followed by a slow 1,500 meters." But Thompson's 1984 times and distances would have won him individual gold medals at the 1912 Games in the 100-meter run, long jump, 400-meter run, 110-meter hurdles, discus throw, pole vault, and javelin throw.

Pick of the Pool

Greg Louganis—springboard and platform king

Only two divers have won the springboard and platform diving events at two different Olympic Games. The first was Patricia McCormick of the United States in 1952 and 1956. The second was fellow American Greg Louganis in 1984 and 1988. Louganis had a tough childhood, but he was so good at diving that he qualified for the 1976 Games when only sixteen years old. On the springboard in 1984, his winning margin of 94 points was the biggest in Olympic history.

Four years later, in Seoul, he hit his head on the springboard during the preliminary round. But he had a doctor stitch it up between rounds and went on to win the final. Then he had to face fourteen-year-old **prodigy** Xiong Ni from China in the platform finals. It was neck and neck until Louganis' last dive, known as the Dive of Death because two men had died trying to make it. Louganis survived and won.

Johnny Weissmuller—king of the water, lord of the apes

As a child, Romanian-born American Johnny Weissmuller was believed to have heart problems. But in 1922, he become the first person to swim the 100-meter freestyle in less than a minute. At the Paris Games of 1924, he won three gold medals. He went on to keep his 100-meter freestyle title at the Amsterdam Games in 1928. His style was extremely relaxed. "I didn't tense up," he explained. After retiring from swimming, he became an actor and starred as Tarzan in many Hollywood movies. Three other Olympic medalists have also played the role!

Mark Spitz—most-golden Olympian

United States swimmer Mark Spitz began his glittering Olympic career at Mexico City in 1968. He returned home with four medals—two gold medals for relays, and a silver and a bronze for individual events. Then four years later at Munich, he rewrote the record books. He won seven gold medals, the most ever won at a single Games. More astonishing still, he won every gold medal with a new world-record time. His father would have been pleased. "Swimming isn't everything," his father told Mark when he was a boy, "winning is."

Dawn Fraser—Australia's greatest Olympian?

Dawn Fraser was only nineteen years old in 1956 when she won her first Olympic 100-meter freestyle title in her home country of Australia. She did it in a world record time of 1 minute 2 seconds, almost 5 seconds faster than the previous Olympic champion. Not bad for someone who had been **asthmatic** as a child, and who was swimming in her first international tournament! At Rome in 1960, having already set a new world record, she successfully defended her Olympic title.

In 1964, the year of the Tokyo Games, she was badly injured in a car accident, but nothing could stop her from competing in her third Olympics. Despite her injuries, she still managed to get in shape for Tokyo. Her training routine included swimming eight miles a day! At 27 years of age, her teammates called her Granny. But her experience paid off in the 100-meter finals when she beat fifteen-year-old American Sharon Stouder to win again, finishing in under a minute! No other Olympic swimmer, male or female, had ever won the same individual event three times in a row.

21

Supreme Strongmen

Alexander Medved—Soviet wrestling sensation

Russian freestyle wrestler Alexander Medved has been called the greatest wrestler of the 20th century or even of the past 2,000 years! The mighty wrestlers of ancient times would probably have found this nimble bear of a man hard to beat. As a light-heavyweight wrestler, and then as a super-heavyweight wrestler, he won three Olympic titles between 1964 and 1972. He also won ten world championships in three weight divisions between 1962 and 1972. Rarely weighing more than his opponent, he won by speed, power, and intelligence.

Naim Suleymanoglu—Turkey's Pocket Hercules

Featherweight weightlifter Naim Suleymanoglu was born in Bulgaria, but his family was Turkish. Although not quite 5 feet (150 centimeters) tall, he was immensely strong. At the age of fourteen, he came within 5 1/2 pounds (2 1/2 kilograms) of breaking the adult world record for combined lifts. By the age of sixteen, he was lifting three times his own body weight. In 1984 he was too young to compete for Bulgaria at the Los Angeles Olympics. Four years later, in 1988, he did compete, but with the Turkish team. This was because in 1986 he **defected**. The government of Bulgaria let him change his nationality after the Turkish government paid a fee of more than $1 milion.

In Seoul he won Turkey's first gold medal in 20 years. Now he was a national hero! He wanted to retire while still at the top, but was persuaded to keep competing. This turned out to be a good idea. He won again in Barcelona and again in Atlanta. He became weightlifting's first triple Olympic champion in three successive Games.

Cassius Clay—the best and the prettiest (or so he said!)

No boxer ever talked or fought a better fight than Cassius Marcellus Clay, winner of the light-heavyweight gold medal at Rome in 1960. Eighteen at the time, Clay was so proud of his medal that he wore it all the time. He even slept with it, so that the gold plating began to come off. He later turned **professional** and won the world heavyweight championship in 1964, before converting to Islam and changing his name to Muhammad Ali. A uniquely talented sportsman, he became one of the world's most famous people during the 1960s and 1970s and lit the Olympic torch at Atlanta in 1996.

Yasuhiro Yamashita—Japan's big fridge!

At almost 6 feet (180 centimeters) in height and weighing 275 pounds (125 kilograms), judo open champion Yasuhiro Yamashita from Japan was described as "a refrigerator with a head on top." After losing in the finals of the Japanese Student Championships in 1977, he did not lose again for 194 national and international matches. He won his Olympic title in 1984 with such a bad leg injury that his opponent had to help him up to the top step to receive his gold medal.

The Flying Housewife

After the 1948 Olympic Games in London, a Dutch athlete named Fanny Blankers-Koen was paraded through Amsterdam in an open coach drawn by four gray horses. Great crowds flocked to see and cheer her. "All I've done is run fast," said the 30-year-old mother of two. "I don't quite see why people should make such a fuss about that." As usual, Mrs. Blankers-Koen was being too modest. She had just become the undisputed star of the London Games. What a rollercoaster ride it was for her there!

Games to brighten the gloom

Between 1936 and 1948 there were no Olympic Games, because of World War II. The war ended in 1945, but so much damage had been done that life was hardly back to normal in Britain by 1948. Food and clothes were still being **rationed**, and many houses had been bombed to rubble. In spite of this, London was to stage the next Games. The organizers made the best of the situation. They spent only $366,000, ignored torrential rains, and housed male athletes in Army camps and female athletes in colleges. One of these women was Fanny Blankers-Koen of the Netherlands.

At Berlin in 1936, eighteen-year-old Fanny seemed to have a glittering Olympic future. But when the 1940 and 1944 Games were canceled, she had no chance to prove herself at the top. By 1948, at age 30, some experts thought she was past her peak.

Over the next eight days, she had four events in which to prove herself. She would compete in the 100-meter run, 80-meter hurdles, 200-meter run, and 4 × 100-meter relay.

Good as gold times four

Fanny's first event was the 100-meter run. She romped home through the mud to win with a time of 11.5 seconds. It equaled her own world record. The 80-meter hurdles came next. After a poor start and hitting the fifth hurdle, she lurched over the line neck-and-neck with Britain's Maureen Gardner. No one knew who had won. As the runners awaited the result, the band began to play the British national anthem. Did that mean Gardner had won? No, it was to mark the arrival of the British royal family, who had just entered the stadium! When the result was announced, Fanny had her second gold medal.

Now the pressure began to build on this great athlete who was lighting up the Games. There was so much talk of her winning three gold medals, that she broke down and nearly pulled out of the 200-meter run altogether. Her husband and coach persuaded her to run, and she finished with the biggest-ever winning margin in a women's 200-meter run finals.

Three events, three golds. The 4 × 100-meter relay was still to come. Fanny ran the last leg of the relay race. When she took the baton, it did not look good. The Dutch team was running fourth. Could she pass three runners in such short a distance? Fanny crossed the finish line to become the first woman to win four **track and field** gold medals. When she got home, her neighbors gave her a bicycle, so that she wouldn't have to run so much.

You Can't Catch Zatopek

Some Olympic champions do not just win, they win in style. The star of the 1952 Games in Helsinki was not a stylist. According to one observer, he ran "like a man who had just been stabbed in the heart." It was also said about him that he "does everything wrong except win." But no one could deny this awkward-looking runner's brilliance. Emil Zatopek was an all-time great.

Going for gold times three

Czech army officer Zatopek arrived at the Helsinki Games in 1952 as the reigning Olympic champion in the 10,000-meter run. In 1948 he had also won a silver medal in the 5,000-meter run. But now he was 30 years old, and he had not been in top form before the Games. Nevertheless, he planned to compete in a third event within eight days in Helsinki. He planned to run the marathon. He had never run a marathon race before, but he believed his tough training methods would work for him.

Emil Zatopek was an incomparable distance runner. Between 1948 and 1954, he won 38 10,000-meter races in a row and often won by huge margins. Years later, he was asked why he looked so pained when he ran. "I was not talented enough to run and smile at the same time," he replied.

His first event was the 10,000-meter run. The rest of the field was strong, but no one else could keep up with Zatopek's blistering pace. He won by about 100 meters. Next up was the 5,000-meter run. It turned out to be one of the most exciting Olympic races ever. Usually in the last lap, Zatopek simply burned off most of his challengers. This time, soon after he kicked for home, three runners stormed past him. This had never happened to him before.

With 250 meters to go, Herbert Schade of Germany, Chris Chataway of Britain, and Alain Mimoun of France looked like they would get the medals. Desperately Zatopek tried to catch up. With 180 meters to go, all four runners were in a line across the track. The head of the runner on the outside of the line was rolling in agony, his arms were thrashing, his chest was heaving. It was Emil Zatopek. 180 meters later, he breasted the finish line tape to win the gold.

"Is it fast enough?"

Later that afternoon, Zatopek heard that his wife, Dana, had just won a gold medal in the javelin throw. "At present," he joked with reporters, "the score of the contest in the Zatopek family is 2–1. This result is too close. To restore some prestige, I will try to improve on the margin in the marathon race." And he did.

Together, Emil Zatopek and his wife Dana won four Olympic gold medals in 1952.

After 9 miles, he was in the lead alongside Britain's Jim Peters. Six weeks before, Peters had run the fastest marathon in history. Zatopek had never run a marathon in his life. He turned to Peters and asked in English, "The pace, is it fast enough?" Peters had started too quickly, and now he felt exhausted. But he did not want Zatopek to know that, so he replied, "No, it's too slow." Zatopek thought about this, then raced ahead to a stunning victory.

Zatopek's triple-gold achievement in Helsinki was magnificent. No one has ever repeated it. Zatopek was not just a brilliant runner and racer, he was a true Olympian, too.

Winter Wonders

Sonja Henie—from skating star to film star

Norway's Sonja Henie was the greatest female figure skater in the world for more than a decade, and she remains the most successful individual woman skater in Olympic history. At the first Winter Olympics in Chamonix, France, in 1924, she was eleven years old. She won no medals at Chamonix, but due to seven hours of training each day, she never lost a competition after the age of thirteen. She was the winner of ten figure skating world championships in a row, and she was also the Olympic gold medalist in 1928, 1932, and 1936. Her **repertoire** was breathtaking, including a spin with as many as 80 revolutions.

In later life she followed a career in the movies, becoming a huge and fabulously wealthy star in the United States. Someone once said, however, that her acting skills were about as good as Charles Laughton's figure skating. Laughton was an actor whose movie roles included the Hunchback of Notre Dame.

Jean-Claude Killy—Killympic hero

The star of the 1968 Winter Olympics at Grenoble, France, was Alpine skier Jean-Claude Killy. In the men's downhill event, in the slalom, and in the giant slalom, the 24-year-old Frenchman turned in gold-medal-winning performances. He became an immensely popular hero in his home country of France. He helped organize the 1992 Winter Games and became a member of the International Olympic Committee in 1995.

Cool runnings

Most Winter Olympic teams come from countries where there is plenty of ice and snow. But at Albertville, France, in 1992, there was a four-man bobsled team from Jamaica. The Jamaicans did not win a medal, but it was a great achievement to qualify for the Games in the first place. The Walt Disney Corporation thought so, too. They made a movie about the team, titled *Cool Runnings*.

Eric Heiden—clean sweep speed skater

At the opening of the 1980 Winter Olympics in Lake Placid, New York, the Olympic oath was taken by Eric Heiden, the 21-year-old U.S. speed skater. He stayed in the headlines by making a clean sweep of the five speed skating gold medals, all in Olympic record times. In the men's 10,000-meter event, he set a new world record. Then his speed-skating sister, Beth, also won a bronze in the women's 3,000-meter event.

Torvill and Dean—incomparable ice dancers

By the time of the 1984 Games in Sarajevo, Britain's Jayne Torvill and Christopher Dean had already been the world ice-dance champions for three years. Their performances at the Olympics then took their sport to a new level of achievement. For their interpretation of the music of Ravel's *Bolero,* all nine judges awarded them the maximum six points for artistic presentation. In the entire competition, they gained twelve sixes out of a possible eighteen.

Glossary

altitude height above sea level

amateur someone who competes for fun, rather than as a job, and who is unpaid

asthmatic suffering from asthma, a disease that affects a person's breathing

Cold War period after World War II of unfriendly relations between the United States and the USSR that never quite became real warfare

communism political, economic, and social system that has state-owned land, factories, and means of production. The USSR became the first communist state in 1917. After World War II, the USSR introduced communism into much of eastern Europe.

decathlon athletic contest made up of the following ten competitive events: 100-meter run, long jump, shot put, high jump, 400-meter run, 110-meter hurdles, discus, pole vault, javelin, 1,500-meter run

defect leave one country to live in another without official permission. During the Cold War, many athletes from Communist countries defected to the West.

endorsement approval of or support for a product in return for money

media plural of medium (of communication), for example newspapers, magazines, TV, and radio

Nazi member or supporter of the National Socialist German Workers' Party, a political party led by Adolf Hitler

phenomenon extraordinary person, thing, or event

prodigy someone, especially a child, who is very talented

professional a paid competitor

rationed when food or other materials, such as gasoline, are given out in limited amounts. There was rationing during and just after World War II.

repertoire the range of skills that a person has

rostrum platform or stage

track and field sporting events that involve running, jumping, throwing, and walking, such as the 100-meter run or the javelin throw

USSR Union of Soviet Socialist Republics, a communist country that included Russia and many smaller nations. The USSR divided into separate countries in 1991.

More Books to Read

Blair, Bonnie, and Greg Brown. *A Winning Edge*. Dallas: Taylor Publishing Company, 1996.

Dheensaw, Cleve, and Deanna Binder. *Celebrate the Spirit: the Olympic Games*. Custer, Wash.: Orca Book Publishers, 1996.

Hunter, Shawn. *Great African Americans in the Olympics*. New York: Crabtree Publishing Company, 1997.

Italia, Robert. *100 Great Moments in the Summer Olympics*. Minneapolis: ABDO Publishing Company, 1996.

———. *100 Great Moments in the Winter Olympics*. Minneapolis: ABDO Publishing Company, 1996.

Index